THE MOMENT BEFORE

CASE FILES: POCKET-SIZED MURDER
MYSTERIES

RACHEL AMPHLETT

SAXON
PUBLISHING

THE MOMENT BEFORE

THE MOMENT BEFORE

Ray Holden cranked open the tinted glass door, then stepped onto the balcony and took a deep breath.

He always loved the view from up here.

At night, he could see the sparkle and flare from the neon signs peppered across the tops of buildings in Canary Wharf while he listened to the laughter and soft clink of glasses from the tables outside the tapas restaurant down the road.

A full moon on the rise would straddle the skyscrapers, bathe the city in a cool light that eased away from the shadows and halted conversations as people paused to stop and stare, raise their phones and try to capture the moment.

This afternoon was different though.

A lethargy seeped into the city suburb, curling its way around the apartment blocks.

Traffic was quiet, save for the occasional delivery truck or cyclist zipping past.

The balconies to either side of him were devoid of life, the neighbours at work or running errands.

The one on his left – owned by a single

woman who worked as a paralegal if his information served him right – held a wrought-iron table and chairs while the glass safety panels were obscured by a variety of herbs growing in colourful pots.

He inhaled the aromas. Basil, oregano, garlic – there was rosemary in there somewhere, too.

He wondered if she cooked, what her signature dish might be.

Something Italian perhaps.

Turning to the balcony on his right, he noticed a discarded off-white teddy bear with one eye missing as it stared up at the blue sky with the other. The glass barrier was covered in stickers, and he wondered which poor sod would have the job of trying to remove those when the family outgrew its home.

Ray's gaze travelled to the park opposite the apartment block at a child's cry.

Two toddlers screeched with delight as they were pushed on swings by their mothers while a commercial airliner banked high in the sky above them as it took off from the city airport.

In the distance, a dog howled as a police siren passed before falling silent.

He wrapped his fingers around the steel guard rail, his knuckles white.

Everything seemed so normal.

And yet—

His doctor told him last week that he needed to relax, quickly followed by a warning that if he didn't, then Ray wouldn't see Christmas because he was so stressed.

His heart couldn't take it.

Ray left the doctor's office and resolved to deal with the stress in his life.

Immediately.

Starting with Joe McAvoy.

Seven years ago, Joe was a zit-covered eighteen-year-old desperate to impress.

After starting as a bartender at one of Ray's nightclubs, he'd quickly risen to the role of supervisor, his smooth delivery of just the right amount of bravado and cheekiness endearing him to Ray.

He'd become like a son, especially to Marcie who was still mourning the fact she couldn't have children twenty years after the news.

Within three years, Ray handed over some of the smaller deals to Joe and watched while the younger man's confidence grew alongside a fearsome reputation that, along with Ray's blessing, forged a partnership that took the business from strength to strength.

But kids didn't always turn out the way you wanted them to, did they?

Ray turned to face the sumptuous living room and loosened his tie as he leaned against the guard rail, the late autumn sun warming the back of his neck.

Inside, the walls were covered with framed posters – old jazz gigs from way back, long before the current tenant had been born. A large black and white photograph of the New York skyline took up the entire space above the television, and he wondered if it was placed there as a goal – or a pipe-dream.

A thick mink-coloured carpet covered the floor,

one that Ray knew cost upwards of five thousand pounds.

Cash, of course.

Because that's how Joe did business.

Safer that way.

Or so he thought.

Running his gaze over the open-plan kitchen and diner, squinting as the gleaming appliances caught the sun, Ray wondered when it started to go wrong.

His ears were still ringing from all the shouting moments earlier. He hated confrontation but it seemed to seek him out on purpose, testing his patience.

Testing his nerves.

Testing his resolve not to reach into his jacket pocket and light up a cig—

No, he wouldn't.

He quit.

A whole week ago, in fact.

When he left the doctor's office.

And without the aid of those little sticky patches that tore the hairs off your arms.

Trying to give up the little white sticks was killing him but Marcie kept nagging and no matter what he did, she could pick up the smell of nicotine on him at fifty paces.

If he were honest, Marcie's rage was a more frightening prospect than cancer.

Ray concentrated on the breathing techniques his doctor had shown him last week and turned back to the street below.

Inhale through the nose over a count of four.

Exhale through the mouth over a count of eight.

There.

Better.

The kids were in their pushchairs now, the mothers nattering away as they walked towards the exit opposite the apartment block, not a care in the world, their laughter drifting up to where he surveyed his kingdom.

A helicopter buzzed across the farthest reaches of the park, its red livery identifying it as a radio station's aircraft as it turned away. High enough not to break any laws, low enough to report on traffic flow in between the advert breaks and chit-chat.

His mobile phone pinged.

Pulling it from his jacket pocket, his eyes skimmed the text.

He says he gave the goods to Mack. Says he got a better price.

Ray's jaw clenched as he eyed the plastic bags on the sofa, the ones containing eighty thousand pounds, all in tens and twenties.

Used.

Money that should have been his.

Joe always had enjoyed the perks of the job.

A little too much.

The expensive suits, the wining and dining, the flash cars.

Despite all that, Joe said he put the money aside, saved it for a rainy day and that the merchandise was still in the warehouse awaiting collection.

The moment before Nick and Neil had taken Joe McAvoy kicking and shouting from the apartment and up the fire escape stairs, Ray almost believed him.

The moment before the text message, he was starting to have doubts.

The moment before, he thought he could trust his business partner.

Ray's thumb hovered over the screen a moment longer, then typed two words.

Do it.

He hit the send button, tucked the phone back in his pocket and sighed.

Seven years.

Seven years they'd been running their drugs operation without a hitch.

Seven years before Joe McAvoy double-crossed him for the first and last time.

Ray inhaled the neighbour's herbs, his fingers twitching towards the crumpled packet in his jacket pocket, the one holding the single cigarette he kept for emergencies.

He heard a shout, the sound of a struggle several floors above McAvoy's apartment.

Pigeons squawked, the beat of panicked wings reminding him of belated applause that echoed off the façade.

A split second later a man's body tumbled past him, right between the two balconies, his expensive suit jacket flapping in the wind.

Speed, mass, a muffled *clang* as McAvoy's forearm caught against the guard rail of the balcony below, then—

Ray didn't watch the body hit the pavement, but he heard it.

Heard the grapefruit-like crush of bones and sinew and skin and muscle as it met concrete.

Heard the screaming begin after the two women with pushchairs turned to see what the noise was.

He closed the floor-to-ceiling glass doors and crossed the plush carpet.

Picked up the plastic bags, testing the weight in his grip, rolling his shoulders to counter the slight tremble in his arm muscles.

Locked the front door, handed the keys to Nick – or was it Neil? Always hard to tell with identical twins.

Followed the twins to the emergency exit stairs. Removed the protective gloves that masked his fingerprints.

Reached the underground car park and climbed in the back of the sleek four-by-four with the smoked glass passenger windows.

Smiled as he removed the last cigarette from the packet and crushed it between his fingers.

The moment before, he was tempted to light it.

The moment before, he remembered his doctor's words.

The moment before, the stress in his life had passed him by.

THE END

ABOUT THE AUTHOR

Rachel Amphlett is a USA Today bestselling author of crime fiction and spy thrillers, many of which have been translated worldwide.

Her novels are available in eBook, print, and audiobook formats from libraries and retailers as well as her website shop.

A keen traveller, Rachel has both Australian and British citizenship.

Find out more about Rachel's books at: www.rachelamphlett.com.

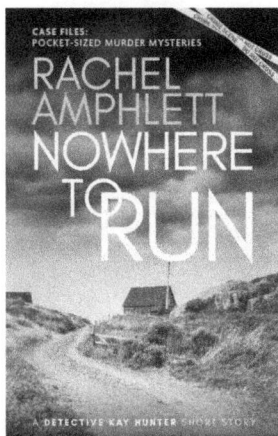

Nowhere to Run

When a series of vicious attacks leaves the local running
community in shock and fear, probationary detective
Kay Hunter is thrust into the middle of a fraught
investigation.

ISBN eBook: 978-1-913498-68-9

ISBN paperback: 978-1-913498-69-6

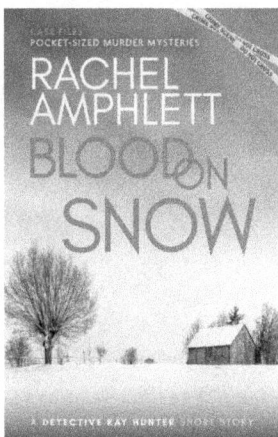

Blood on Snow

A suburban housewife is found dead in her
garden. There is no weapon, no witnesses, and the
only set of footprints belong to her cat.

Probationary detective Kay Hunter and her
colleagues are convinced it's murder – but how can
they find a killer when there are no clues?

ISBN eBook: 978-1-913498-70-2
ISBN paperback: 978-1-913498-71-9

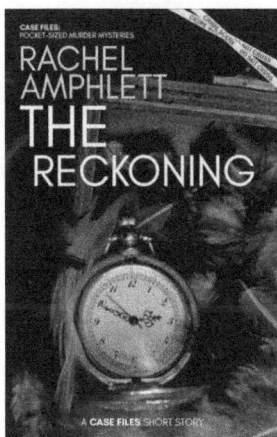

The Reckoning

The newest arrival at a care home for the elderly
carries an air of mystery that even an ex-WW2
Resistance fighter can't help trying to solve.

Then matters take a sinister turn…

ISBN eBook: 978-1-913498-70-2
ISBN paperback: 978-1-913498-71-9

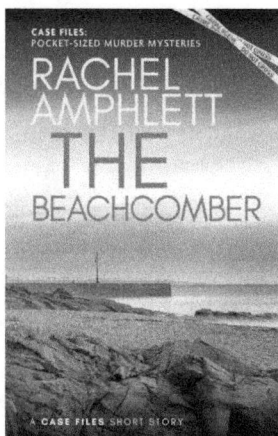

The Beachcomber

Staying at a tiny guesthouse in Cornwall after the summer, Julie spends her days combing the beaches, looking for things to collect while hiding from her past. Then a storm breaks, and suddenly she's scared.

Because you never know what might wash up after a storm…

ISBN eBook: 978-1-913498-93-1
ISBN paperback: 978-1-913498-94-8

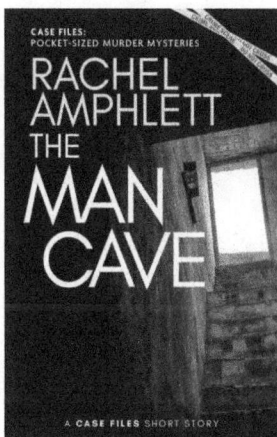

The Man Cave

When Darren regains consciousness in a dank
basement, escape turns out to be the least of his
worries...

ISBN eBook: 978-1-913498-96-2
ISBN paperback: 978-1-913498-97-9

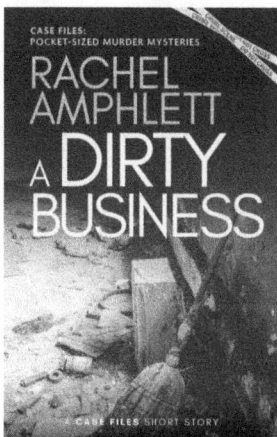

A Dirty Business

When Michael arrives at work early one winter's
day, he discovers that he's not the only one who's
had a busy morning...

ISBN eBook: 978-1-913498-98-6
ISBN paperback: 978-1-913498-99-3

CPSIA information can be obtained
at www.ICGtesting.com
Printed in the USA
BVHW041345311022
650735BV00007B/213

9 781915 231178